# TIPTOES WINS THROUGH

IRENE BYERS

# Tiptoes wins through

*Illustrated by Lynette Hemmant*

**HODDER AND STOUGHTON**
**LONDON  SYDNEY  AUCKLAND  TORONTO**

*For Stephanie and Graham*

ISBN 0-340-19611-4

First published 1976
Second impression 1987

Published by Hodder and Stoughton Children's Books,
a division of Hodder and Stoughton Ltd,
Mill Road, Dunton Green, Sevenoaks, Kent TN13 2YJ

Printed in Great Britain by T. J. Press (Padstow) Ltd,
Padstow, Cornwall

# CONTENTS

# 1
# Shock for Timothy

'For the last time, Tim, I'm asking you to take your pigeon off the breakfast table.'

Timothy shot his mother a reproachful glance. 'Oh, Mum. Tiptoes is hungry. And it *is* his last meal here.'

Mrs Marshall poured out a cup of tea and handed it to Gran who was sitting at the head of the table. 'It makes no difference. I will not have Tiptoes strutting among the cornflakes and kippers. It's unhealthy.'

'Tiptoes isn't strutting.' Timothy's reply was indignant. 'And he isn't unhealthy.' Capturing his pet, he spread out a grey-blue wing. 'Look at the bloom on his feathers and see how bright his eyes are.'

His mother put down her cup with a little bang. 'I've far too much on my mind to bother about your pigeon's finer points. The removal men will be here in less than an hour and we haven't even finished breakfast.'

'Gosh, yes!' cried Tim, as if this were news to him.

'To think that by tonight Tiptoes' loft will be in a real garden instead of a rotten old back yard. Where's Dad? I want to be sure he doesn't forget to take it down for me.'

'He's already gone to the . . .' Timothy's mother stopped short. Gran looked at her steadily. 'You're not being fair to the lad, Alice. You'd best tell him now as later. I never did hold with keeping it back in the first place.'

'Keeping what back?' Timothy looked uneasily from one to the other. 'What's Gran getting at, Mum?'

Mrs Marshall sighed. 'Simply this, Tim. We . . . we aren't moving to a Council house as we'd hoped, but to another flat.'

'Like . . . like this?' Timothy's voice faltered as he looked round the semi-basement kitchen, which in spite of his parents' efforts always seemed so gloomy.

'Much better than this,' continued his mother. 'It's got central heating, a lovely large kitchen, three bed-rooms and a sitting-room with such big windows that you can see half across London. And we'll be able to grow flowers on the balcony.'

'Balcony!' echoed Timothy. 'I don't understand. You mean there isn't a garden, not even a back yard?'

His mother fell silent and it was his grandmother who

answered. 'You'd best face it, Tim. We're going to live in one of them skyscraper buildings. Never thought I'd end my days fifteen floors up towards the moon. Fair gives me palpitations just to think of it.'

'Fifteen floors up!' Timothy caught up his pigeon and, holding it close to his chest, he backed away from the table. His eyes were clouded with misery. 'You lied to me, all of you. You said we were going to a house. What's Tiptoes going to do if there isn't a garden for his loft? I won't go. I won't.'

Mrs Marshall put her hands to her head. 'Oh, Tim, don't carry on so. No one lied to you. We just couldn't bring ourselves to tell you until we had to. Don't you see? We had no other choice. With the demolition men only four houses away, we had to take what the Council offered. If we hadn't, we'd have been homeless.'

'We could have gone to a boarding house for a time like Bob's father and mother did. The landlady let him keep his pigeon.'

'Your dad doesn't earn that sort of money,' said his mother. 'I know you're disappointed, but please don't look so miserable. We'll solve the problem somehow.'

Timothy did not answer. The knot of disappointment still hung like a leaden weight in his chest. He knew now why his father and mother had always found some reason to prevent him from visiting the new home, and why Gran had always looked so disapproving. As if sensing she had not convinced him, his mother went on: 'What's more, we're not moving far, only three blocks away, so you'll be able to keep in touch with the pet shop owner, Mr Brent, and take Tiptoes for trial flights. Doesn't that make you feel happier?'

'No, it doesn't.'

'Then you'd best take your thoughts off it by clearing up some of the muddle in your bedroom,' retorted his mother, beginning to clear the table. 'There's a mountain of comics you can put in the dustbin for a start. I mean it, Tim. Stop moping.'

Timothy did not immediately obey his mother. Instead, he went out into the yard and put Tiptoes in his carrying basket. Next he filled a small zinc trough with water and hung it on the side so that the pigeon could drink through the bars. His mother simply did not understand, he decided. After the roominess of his loft, Tiptoes would hate spending even one night in so small a space. His one hope lay with his father.

Mr Marshall was almost as interested in the pigeon as Timothy was, so perhaps he would be able to persuade the removal men to sell him a packing case. Turned on its side and a length of chicken wire fixed across the front, it would do quite well as a temporary shelter. And between his bus driving shifts, his father would soon be able to build another loft.

With these immediate problems resolved to his satisfaction, Timothy set about his tasks willingly enough, and by the time the removal men arrived, he was almost cheerful.

They were big, broad-shouldered men with loud voices and they were extremely skilful at handling even the most awkward pieces of furniture. Timothy stood in the yard again and thought how shabby their possessions looked against the brilliant whiteness of the new refrigerator his father had managed to buy out of his overtime pay.

His thoughts raced to the future. One day when Tiptoes was fully trained and won a really important race, he, too, might have money to spare. Sometimes the prizes were big, Mr Brent had told him. Or he might win a silver cup. His mother would be pleased because she was always complaining that the sideboard looked a bit bare.

Day-dreaming in this way, Timothy was unaware of the thin drizzle that had begun to fall, until his father's sharp voice reminded him.

'Can't you find something better to do than stand there getting soaked, Tim?' he snapped. 'You'd best get into the Mini and stay there.' Timothy put on his macintosh, stuffed a bag of maple peas into his pocket, then eased himself and the carrying basket into the back seat of the little red car.

A quarter of an hour later, with the doors bolted and barred, the removal van moved away. The family car also edged its way from the kerb. In no time, it seemed, they were driving along a concrete slipway and coming to a stop outside the front entrance of Peacock Building. Timothy's mother got out, closely followed by the rest of the family. All four looked up.

The mammoth building, with its hundreds of windows looking like glass eyes, was as grey and as uninviting as the November sky. Doubts and fears crowded in on Timothy again, and he did not feel any happier when Gran snorted and said, 'Peacock Building indeed. The only bit of colour I can see comes from that line of washing hanging up there. Do you know what it reminds me of? A huge filing cabinet.'

'Gran!' Timothy's mother shot her a warning glance.

'All right, all right, Alice. I'll say no more except to warn you that if I don't like it, I won't stay. I'll go into an old people's home.'

Fortunately Timothy's attention had wandered. He was wondering which of the stone balconies would be theirs. But before he could count to the fifteenth floor, he found himself gently propelled towards the entrance hall. His mother looked at the two lifts. One served the floors with odd numbers and the other the floors with even numbers. She pressed the button for the odd-numbers lift. No reassuring indicator light winked at her. She tried again, and as she did so a woman came out of the second lift.

'You're wasting your time on that one,' she said. 'The odd-numbers lift hasn't worked for a month. It's them kids from Baltimore Block. They make-believe the lift is a rocket, you see, and when theirs breaks down, they come and do ours in.'

Mrs Marshall looked at her in dismay. 'Then whatever shall we do? We're about to move into number eighty-one.'

The woman shrugged her shoulders. 'Same as everyone else has to. You can either winch the furniture up, or take the even lift to the floor above and walk down a flight.' She grinned. 'You get there in the end, but it's hard on the feet, and I don't envy you with the removal men.'

No truer word was ever said, for when the disastrous

news was broken to them, they dumped the settee in the foyer and sat down on it.

'Sorry, Missis,' said the foreman. 'This sort of lark wasn't in the contract. Perishing kids. I know what I'd do to their backsides if I lived here.'

While his mother and Gran pleaded, Timothy stood silent. In his heart there lurked the wild hope that they might be forced to return to the old home. His father, however, who was already aware of the crisis, solved it by pressing a five pound note into the foreman's hands, and promising more when the job was finished.

'Blackmail! That's what it is,' muttered Gran. 'Workmen ought to take the rough with the smooth same as we have to.'

Mr Marshall pressed the button to the sixteenth floor. 'Pipe down, Gran, or we *will* have a strike on our hands.'

Timothy felt his stomach lurch at the lift's upward thrust, but when the doors opened he could hardly believe that they had risen to the sixteenth floor. There was no sensation of height until they went into their new flat and stood before the sitting-room window. The view from there was breath-taking, but Timothy had no eyes for London's famous buildings or for the far away heights of Greenwich. His gaze was fixed on the stone balcony. It was smaller than he had imagined, but it could just about hold a pigeon loft, he decided. Turning away he said to his father, 'Do you think we could keep one of the packing cases?'

'What for?'

'For his precious pigeon, of course,' replied Gran, shrinking back from the window. 'Oh, lor'. My heart's going nineteen to the dozen. I'll never get used to it. Never.'

'Oh, Gran, of course you will.' Mrs Marshall eased her gently on to the first of the packing cases. 'You sit there and as soon as I can lay my hands on the kettle, I'll make us all a nice cup of tea.' She looked down as she felt a tug at her arm. 'What is it now, Tim?'

'Dad hasn't answered my question. If I can't have a packing case where will Tiptoes sleep tonight?'

'Tiptoes! Tiptoes!' cried his mother impatiently. 'That's all I've heard from you since you got up this morning. It'll be time enough to think of him when we've got our own beds up. So not another word unless you want me to be really cross with you.'

Timothy picked up his carrying basket and slouched out of the flat. He felt rebellious and hurt by his parents' indifference. He was also a little afraid. Why wouldn't either of them give him a direct answer about Tiptoes? As he reached the corridor he almost collided with a boy. He was tall and thin and considerably older than Timothy.

'Hi yer,' he called out. 'Haven't seen you around before.'

'We're just moving in,' mumbled Timothy.

'What you got in there?' The boy pointed to the carrying basket.

'My pet pigeon. He's called Tiptoes and I'm training him to be a racer. I'm going to try and find a box or something for him to sleep in tonight.'

The boy grinned and ran a hand through his unkempt reddish-coloured hair. 'Take care old Smithers, the caretaker, doesn't catch you then.'

'Why?'

'Hasn't anyone told you? Pets aren't allowed in the flats. I got caught good and proper when we moved in. Had to have my cat done in. But it's all there in the small print of your rent book. The only pet you'll ever be able to keep is a goldfish.'

'I don't believe you. My dad would have told me.'

'Not if he knew you'd be upset. He'd want you to get settled in first, then sort of break the news gently. Grown-ups are like that.'

Timothy did not want to believe the boy. Yet every word had the ring of truth. It explained why his father and mother would not answer questions and why his mother had been so impatient. They had known all the time.

## 2
# Timothy runs away

Timothy did not wait to hear more. He had no clear plan in his mind, but as his feet pounded down flight after flight of concrete steps, his one resolve was to take Tiptoes as far away from the hateful block of flats as he could.

Outside the thin drizzle of rain had turned to a steady downpour. But it did not deter him. Pulling up the collar of his macintosh Timothy ran along the slipway and did not slow down until the fear of bruising his pigeon forced him to a jogtrot. Suddenly, as he rounded the corner and entered the main road, he bumped into a girl. She had small features, big blue eyes and fair, shoulder-length hair. It was his school friend Betty.

'Hi, Tim, where are you off to?' she asked in surprise. 'I thought you were moving today.' She fell into step beside him. 'I was just coming to see if I could help. Is anything the matter?'

'Push off and leave me alone,' Timothy said gruffly. 'I don't want you or anyone else tagging along.'

Betty took no notice. She was used to Timothy's moods. 'So that's it. You've found out. You're upset about Tiptoes.'

Timothy stopped and glared at her. 'Do you mean to say you knew about pets not being allowed in the flats, too? Why didn't you warn me?'

'I didn't know, until I heard mum and dad talking about him this morning. They were awfully upset. I bet your mum and dad are too.'

'No, they're not.' Timothy kicked at an empty tin. 'But I know one thing. If there's no home for Tiptoes, there's no home for me either.'

Betty's eyes grew rounder. 'You mean you're running

away? Oh, Tim, you can't. Have you got any food or money or anything?'

Timothy looked stubborn. 'No, but it doesn't matter. I won't go back. I'll just walk and walk until I think of something.'

'Silly! You can't walk all night. You'd only be nabbed by a policeman.' Betty gave a hop and a skip to keep up with him, and her face suddenly looked thoughtful. 'I believe I know a place where you could hide – for the time being, I mean.'

'Where?'

'There's a hut on the allotments. In summer the tools are kept there, but now that it's winter no one uses it.'

'Won't the door be locked?'

Betty nodded. 'But my dad has the key and I know where he keeps it.'

'You mean you'd pinch it?'

Again Betty nodded. 'I'll bring you some food, too, and a couple of thick pullovers to wear during the night.'

Timothy's spirits rose only to fall again. 'Oh, what's the use. You're bound to be caught.'

'No, I won't. Mum and dad always watch the telly on Saturday evening. Never move from it.' She grinned. 'I'll bring a torch and flash it twice. Then you'll know it's me.'

21

Timothy was sensible enough to know that he ought not to involve Betty, but at the same time he realised that he didn't have any choice. He had rushed into this adventure without thought, and November nights were long and cold. Furthermore, he was already feeling hungry.

The entrance to the allotments lay at the far end of the small park where he and Betty had so often taken Tiptoes for short training flights. Timothy waited until a couple of passers-by had vanished from sight, then

begging Betty not to be long, he squeezed through a gap in the almost leafless hedge.

The neat orderliness of summer had gone. On one or two plots a few winter cabbages struggled for survival. On others the brown but still feathery tops of carrots nodded to the odd clump of Brussels sprouts. Picking a leaf or two from a cabbage, Timothy hurried towards the shed. As Betty had said, the door was securely locked, but his exploring fingers soon found that the bar holding a fanlight type of window into position was broken. Swinging it wide, he propped the window open with a long stick and placed his carrying basket on the shelf inside. A minute later he had swung himself up and squeezed through the opening.

Once inside he looked round the shed. It was stoutly built and dry, and smelt strongly of earth and compost. In the middle of the floor stood a table, and propped against a store cupboard was a wooden crate with a widely slatted lid. Timothy almost cheered. Not only was it large, but it was lined with fine wood shavings. In no time he had transferred Tiptoes to this makeshift nesting box. Then, having given his pigeon a handful of maple peas and a cabbage leaf, he sat down to begin his vigil.

It was a long one, and as his wrist watch ticked away the hours he was more and more certain that Betty had failed him. To bolster his waning courage he told stories to himself and sang some of his school songs.

But the gathering darkness and his increasing hunger did not help, while the wind whining through the nearby trees added to his sense of loneliness. By six o'clock, when he had resigned himself to a supper of raw carrots, and was on the point of climbing out, a light flashed close to the window. The next instant the key turned in the lock and Betty was beside him.

Timothy sighed with relief. 'I thought you were never coming.'

Betty flashed the torch round. 'At least you found your own way inside. I couldn't get here any sooner. Uncle Bob called in unexpectedly and stayed and stayed.'

Timothy took a deep breath, then said hopefully: 'Do I smell chips?'

'And fried fish. Uncle Bob gave me fifty pence, so I didn't have to raid Mum's larder.' Sitting on the floor beside him, Betty shared out the contents of the newspaper-wrapped parcel. Timothy thought no food had ever tasted so good, and when the last morsel was eaten, he felt both sleepy and content. Betty, too, would have curled up in a corner, but Timothy insisted that she returned home at once.

'Oh, Tim, don't send me away,' she pleaded. 'We always share things together. And the hut *was* my idea.'

'You must go.' Timothy was firm. 'We don't want the police looking for two of us. Besides, your mum would never forgive me if you stayed out all night.'

Betty wanted to argue, but she knew that Timothy was right. This was one adventure she could not share to the full. So leaving behind the two heavy pullovers, a spare torch, and the promise that she would be back with breakfast in the morning, she groped her way along the muddy path between the allotments.

Alone once more, Timothy shone the torch on his pigeon. The golden-rimmed eyes blinked up at him, then closed. Satisfied that his pet was fed and comfortable, Timothy put on the two pullovers, then lay on the floor and rested his head against the wooden crate.

Very soon he was asleep and dreaming that Tiptoes had won a cross-Channel race. But as Timothy stepped up to the platform to receive the award, the silver cup grew heavier and heavier in his hands. Someone, too, was tapping him on the shoulder as if reprimanding him. Timothy stirred in his sleep and turned over. His head slipped off the packing case and hit the floor. The shock roused him. For a moment he stared stupidly upwards thinking that Betty had come back. Then as the figure bending over him straightened and shone the torch on himself, he saw that it was not Betty but Mr Brent, the pet shop owner. Rain had plastered his greying hair to his forehead, and his mouth was unsmiling. But the eyes beneath the heavy brows were compassionate.

'Well, Tim,' he began, 'this is an odd place to find ourselves on a cold, wet Saturday evening.'

Timothy struggled to a sitting position. In spite of the two pullovers he felt cramped and chilled. 'How . . . how did you know where to find me?' His voice rose. 'Oh, I can guess. Betty ratted on me. The rotten little twister. I'll never speak to her again.'

'No one ratted on you, lad.' Mr Brent squatted on his heels. 'I'd been round to your home and found your mum and dad and gran in a fine old state. Didn't stop to think how they would feel, did you? The least I could do was to offer to help your dad to search out some of your old haunts. And quite by chance I bumped into Betty as she entered her front gate. She was carrying a bunch of carrots. And that set me wondering why she had visited the allotments on a wet, winter's evening. In fact I asked her. Your Betty's clever. She thought up a very convincing answer, but unfortunately she dropped a key. It didn't belong to any front door. Then I remembered this hut, and putting two and two together, the answer I came up with was one small boy and a pet pigeon.'

'All right, so you've found me. But if you make me go back, I'll only run away again.'

'Fair enough, if you don't like what we've arranged between us.'

Timothy's mouth took on the familiar stubborn curve. 'What could anyone arrange? Mum and dad put up a good pretence. But they knew all the time that pets weren't allowed in the flats. So if you're thinking of offering me a goldfish instead, you can fry it for breakfast.'

Mr Brent stood up again. 'No, but I *was* thinking of offering a home for Tiptoes among my own pigeons. In fact it had already been decided between your dad and me, and I thought he had told you. Evidently he decided the good news should come from me. That's why he stalled a bit when you began worrying him about Tiptoes. I must say, though, Tim, I'm surprised you didn't come to me in the first place instead of staging this run away act.'

'I would have,' said Timothy, 'only I thought you were mad at me when the pigeon you gave me as a mate for Tiptoes died two weeks ago.'

'I wasn't angry. Pigeons get sick just as you and I do. I was only sorry I couldn't cure her. Well, Tim, what do you think of my offer?'

Timothy's brown eyes shone. 'Smashing! I'll look after him myself, and I'll do any amount of jobs for you in my spare time to help pay for his keep.'

'You'll have to do even more, Tim,' Mr Brent smiled. 'I've always believed that Tiptoes would make a good racer, but if he's to succeed, you'll have to train him even harder than you did before. It all depends on you, Tim.'

'And on Tiptoes,' added Timothy.

# 3
# Clash in the corridor

When Timothy got home after surrendering Tiptoes into Mr Brent's safe keeping, he expected a severe scolding from his parents. To his surprise they did not refer to his escapade. On the other hand, Gran demanded the full story. So when he had had a hot bath and was sitting up in bed drinking a glass of hot milk he told her everything. Gran listened quietly, then she said: 'So your little problem solved itself nicely, Tim, but it mightn't have. You could have been nabbed for breaking and entering and Tiptoes might have died from exposure.'

'Come off it, Gran,' Timothy said scornfully. 'I'd never take risks with Tiptoes. The packing case was snug enough. You're trying to scare me.'

'No, I'm not, but you've got to learn that running away from problems never solves a thing. Leastways, that's what I was brought up to believe.' She smiled and her grey eyes twinkled. 'Not that I'd mind a chance to run away from this dump. Only trouble is my legs won't carry me far or fast enough these days.'

Timothy put down his glass and gave her a hug. 'Oh, Gran, it may not be as bad as you think. You don't get the feeling of height indoors.'

'No, but you do from the balcony.' She sighed. 'The old place wasn't much, but at least you could have a chat over the fence.'

'With all these people living in the block, you'll soon make new friends.'

'Seems you've made one already.' Gran poked a hair pin back into place. 'A boy called Jake knocked earlier to ask if you'd come back. That's how we first knew you'd run off.'

'Did he have reddish hair, and was he wearing patched blue jeans?'

Gran nodded. 'That's right. You sound as if you don't like him.'

'I dunno whether I do or don't.' Timothy snuggled beneath the bedclothes. 'I expect he's all right, but he needn't have looked so pleased when he told me no pets were allowed in the flats.'

Timothy woke early the next morning. The bright kitchen with its shining steel sink and its numerous wall cupboards was strange to him, but at length, after a search, he found a packet of cornflakes and managed to boil himself an egg. Half way through the meal his mother appeared. 'Good gracious!' she exclaimed. 'What's the hurry? I thought you'd sleep late after last night.'

Timothy's cheeks turned a little pink. 'I'm sorry I worried you, but this morning I've got to go and look after Tiptoes and clean out the loft for Mr Brent. I can, can't I, Mum?'

'I suppose so.' Mrs Marshall gave him an affectionate glance. 'I'm sorry about last night too. Neither your dad nor I handled the matter of Tiptoes very well.' She filled the kettle. 'But no being late for dinner, mind. You've got lots of things to sort out in your bedroom this afternoon.'

'All right, Mum.' Timothy finished his second slice

of bread and butter, glanced out of the window to see what the weather was like, then made for the corridor and ran down the flight of stairs to the lift that was working. A boy stood in front of the closed gates. It was Jake.

'Good,' he began. 'Glad you could make it. We're picking up Sam and Nobby on the fourth floor.'

'What for?' asked Timothy, completely mystified.

'Didn't the old girl tell you?'

'Do you mean my gran?'

'Is that who she is? I told her I was taking you to meet the gang this morning. We've got a smashing hide-out in the basement of an empty warehouse on Maybury Street. The police keep their peepers on it, but they've never caught us yet.' As he said this the lift drew level and the doors opened. Jake waited for Timothy to enter, but Timothy shook his head.

'Sorry, Jake, nothing doing. Even if Gran had given me the message, I couldn't have come. I've got a date with my pigeon.'

Jake's eyes widened. 'You mean you pulled a fast one on old Smithers? Where are you hiding it? In the clothes drying area?'

'Not likely,' said Timothy. 'A pigeon fancier friend of mine has given me a home for him. But he's still my pigeon and I've got to look after him.'

'Aren't you the lucky one,' replied Jake. 'No pal turned up in time to save my cat. But your pigeon can wait. It isn't everyone who gets into the gang on his first day in Peacock Building. We're choosy. But it so happens we need another look-out. So come on. Don't let's waste any more time.'

Timothy broke free from the bigger boy's grip. In spite of his apparent friendliness, there was something about Jake that made him feel uneasy. 'I've told you once,' he said firmly. 'There's nothing doing this morning.' And with that Timothy turned and ran down the stairs.

He met no one until he reached the fourth floor. Here to his dismay he was again confronted by Jake, who had used the lift, and two other boys whom he took to be Nobby and Sam. Slowly they advanced towards him.

'This is him,' said Jake, all trace of friendliness gone from his voice. 'Turned me down flat because of his mouldy pigeon. And me offering him a place in the gang too.'

'What say we help him change his mind,' said one of the other boys.

Timothy felt his temper rise. 'Oh, drop dead the lot

of you,' he burst out. 'If I don't want to join your beastly gang, I don't. And there's nothing you can do about it.'

'That's what you think,' said the third boy. He turned to Jake. 'Looks a bit like a puffed-out pigeon himself, doesn't he?'

Jake grinned. 'Let's see if he's got the homing instinct as well.' So saying, he landed a punch on Timothy's right eye. Timothy reeled back, then recovering, retaliated with a wild swing to the nearest chin. But the odds were too heavily weighted against him. In a matter of seconds he was flat on the ground with Jake sitting astride him, and his arms pinioned by the other boys.

'Now will you change your mind?' asked Jake. 'It's your last chance.'

Timothy's eye hurt and his mouth was cut and swollen from coming into contact with a hard head. Nevertheless, he still had some spirit left.

'I will not.' Kicking out with both legs, he shouted at the top of his voice. Help came unexpectedly. The lift door opened, and Gran, umbrella at the ready, charged at the sprawling heap of boys. A couple of whacks brought a yelp from Jake and Sam. A third sent Nobby rolling against the wall. All three glared up at the old lady.

'Plenty more where those came from,' she shouted. 'Think you lot want teaching what's fair in a fight. Now be off with you or you'll have another taste.' She swung the umbrella in the air. The boys rose and, with the equally timely appearance of the caretaker, scurried for the ground floor. Timothy also rose to his feet. 'Thanks a lot, Gran. What were you doing in the lift?'

'Trying the perishing thing out. Got to get some courage from somewhere. But all those buttons scare the daylight out of me. Lucky for you I pressed the wrong one. Young hooligans.'

'Are you coming down with me?' Tim still felt badly in need of an ally.

The old lady shook her head. 'Had enough for one day already.' She swung round on the caretaker. 'It's your job to keep order on the stairs, isn't it?'

Mr Smithers nodded. 'But you don't know what you're asking, lady. What was the trouble? Testing you out, were they?' he added, looking at Timothy. 'Don't suppose they meant any real harm. But seeing as you're a newcomer, I'd best see you off the premises. Never know where those young devils might be lurking. Not going to play nursemaid to you all the time, mind.'

The caretaker was as good as his word, and to Timothy's relief no one lurked in the entrance hall or on the slipway. Thanking Mr Smithers, he hurried to the pet shop as fast as he could. By the time he arrived at the primrose-painted door that led to the flat above the shop, he had almost forgotten his unfortunate encounter.

Mr Brent was quick to answer the bell. Although he gave Timothy a searching glance, he did not immediately refer to the boy's dishevelled appearance. Putting on a protective white coat and handing another to Timothy, he led the way to the large yard at the rear of the premises. Then swinging the boy round to face him, he said: 'Accident or fight, Tim?'

'Neither,' replied Tim. 'You can't call three against one a fight.' Briefly he told Mr Brent of his clash on the fourth-floor corridor. 'And all because I didn't want to join their rotten gang.'

Mr Brent looked thoughtful. 'And one of the boys you think was called Sam. Odd he should have turned against you. He's supposed to be keen on pigeons himself. His father's one of the most successful racers in the neighbourhood. Won any number of prizes. Pity, Tim. Seems you've run into a load of trouble today.'

'What else?' Timothy asked the pet shop owner anxiously. 'Tiptoes hasn't flown away, has he?'

'I doubt if he'd want to fly to the nearest tree this morning.' Ignoring the main section of the well-built wooden loft with its landing platforms and little hinged flaps that allowed the homing pigeons to enter of their own free will, Mr Brent went to a smaller one which normally housed his very young birds. This, like the main loft, was divided into compartments, but only one was occupied. Below on the floor a scatter of maple peas lay uneaten. In the lantern-shaped drinking trough, the water was at rim level.

Timothy gazed up at his pet. The golden-rimmed eyes were shut; the silver grey head was huddled into the breast feathers.

'What's the matter with him?' he asked fearfully.

'He's caught what we fanciers call a one-eyed cold. It's a common enough complaint among pigeons. That shed on the allotments must have been more draughty than you thought, Tim.'

'Is it serious?' Timothy's heart missed a beat as he thought of the hen pigeon that had already died.

'Not if it's treated in time.' Mr Brent took a bottle from his pocket and added some of the liquid to the drinking water. 'This should help. Don't worry. Tiptoes is young and healthy. In two or three days' time he'll be ready to start training.'

# 4
## The hideout

Timothy worked hard that morning. He cleaned out the main pigeon loft. He chopped up lettuce and watercress and mixed it with a little salt. Next he filled the bathing trough in the yard and watched while Mr Brent rationed out the maple peas and tic beans. Now and again he peered into the loft which housed his sick pigeon, but although he once caught Tiptoes taking a sip of water, there did not seem to be any improvement in his condition.

'Stop worrying, Tim,' said Mr Brent. 'I tell you, he'll be all right. Hand me the bag of oyster shell health grit.'

Timothy knew that oyster shell grit was good for pigeons, but he thought the pet shop owner was being over generous with the peas and the greenstuff. 'Aren't you giving them rather a lot to eat?' he remarked.

Mr Brent tossed in another handful. 'You always feed pigeons heavily until the end of the moulting season. Then after Christmas we cut down a bit. Hens won't lay if they are too fat.' He bent closer to the feeding birds. 'Which do you like best?' he asked. 'The Red Grizzles, the Checquers or the Pieds?'

Timothy confessed that he did not know one bird from another, but added that the blue one with the blackish feathers was a little beauty.

Mr Brent went into the loft and picked her up. 'You've got a good eye, Tim. She's a Checquer.' He spread out a wing. 'Good tight feathering, clean eyes and dry, clean feet. All points to look for.'

'Has she raced yet?'

'Many times, but only on the short runs so far. Would you like to have her, Tim?'

'You mean as a mate for Tiptoes? Gosh! I can't wait for him to get better.'

'Not so fast, my young pigeon fancier. Have you forgotten? We don't pair up pigeons until St Valentine's Day. Meanwhile we've got to get Tiptoes used to his new surroundings. So when he *is* better, we'll let him fly with some of the older birds, but not until your second pigeon has been ringed and registered at the club.'

'Why?'

Mr Brent looked a little stern. 'Have you forgotten so soon? You can't race pigeons until they're ringed and registered and the details sent to the Royal National Homing Union. By the way, are you going to give your second pigeon a name, too?'

Timothy thought for a moment. 'I shall call her Blue Haze. I think it suits her. Gosh! If either of them got lost, I think I'd give up.'

Mr Brent restored the bird to her loft. 'No, you wouldn't. You'd start again. Do you know, Tim, that twenty-three of my pigeons went adrift last year. Only two of those returned after an absence of three months.

One had hit a pylon and only just made it. It flopped on to this landing platform with its chest ripped open.'

Timothy swallowed hard. 'Ugh! Poor thing. Did it die?'

'No, I simply pushed its gullet back into place and left the bird to heal itself. In a month it was flying again.'

'Who are you kidding?'

Mr Brent shook his head. 'I'm trying to tell you that pigeons are tough. Tiptoes' one-eyed cold is nothing. Now be off with you, and if you have any more trouble with Jake, Sam or Nobby, let me know and I'll give Constable Rogers the tip-off. The trouble with these lads is that they haven't any means of letting off steam. Pity we can't turn them all into pigeon fanciers.'

Timothy returned to Peacock Building much happier than when he set out. He even had confidence to press the lift button and walk down from the sixteenth floor. As he did so, Sam emerged from the clothes drying area. Timothy ignored him and walked on. Sam caught him up. 'Hey, give a feller a chance, will you?' he said.

'Why should I?'

'No reason.' Sam scuffed one shoe against the other. 'Oh, can't you see I'm trying to say I'm sorry about what happened earlier on? That goes for Jake, too. We want to make it up to you.'

'Don't make me laugh.'

'No, honest, it's Jake's idea. We're having a binge in the warehouse this evening. We each bring something to eat and drink, only you won't have to because you're going to be a sort of guest of honour.' He grinned. 'So you'll come, won't you?'

Timothy thought for a moment. 'I might.'

Sam shifted his gaze a little. 'Good. There's just one thing. Every new guy has to go through a kind of ceremony first. It makes you one of us.'

'What kind of ceremony?'

'Nothing to be scared of. Jake will explain when you get there. I'll call for you about six.'

'All right.' Timothy let himself into the flat with the key his mother had given him, and went straight to the bathroom. But no amount of bathing lessened the discoloration round his right eye. Dabbing it with talcum powder, he joined his mother in the kitchen. The joint she was taking out of the oven smelt delicious. She at once noticed the damage to his eye. 'It's nothing, Mum,' said Tim, interrupting her. 'It looks worse than it is. I bumped into something.'

Gran winked at him. 'Or did something bump into you?'

'Was it a scrap, Tim?' asked his mother anxiously.

'A boy called Sam knocked a short time ago. He seemed mighty anxious to see you.'

'I've just met him.' Timothy licked the gravy spoon. 'He wants me to go to a party this evening.' He was not at all sure that he wanted to go, but if he did not make friends soon, life in the big block of flats would be very lonely. 'Can I go, Mum?'

Mrs Marshall filled a tureen with vegetables. 'I don't see why not. I'm glad you've made friends so quickly. How was Tiptoes?'

'He's got a one-eyed cold.'

'A one-eyed what!' exclaimed his mother. 'The phrases you use, Tim.'

'It's what pigeon fanciers call it, and it isn't serious. On St Valentine's Day he's going to be paired with a hen called Blue Haze, then they'll have babies and —'

'Stop, Tim, stop,' implored his mother. 'When you gabble like that I can't take in a thing.'

During lunch Timothy repeated his news more slowly and when the meal was over and he had helped with the washing-up, he spent the rest of the afternoon reading a book on pigeon rearing. At half past five he remembered the party and, putting his book away, he went into his bedroom and stared in amusement at the coloured shirt and best suit his mother had laid out for him. Ten minutes later, wearing a thick pullover and a stout pair of rubber-soled shoes, he called good-bye to his parents, who were watching television, and set out with Sam.

Once free of the lighted slipway, his companion turned and twisted through side streets. The half-demolished houses looked ghostly against the starlit sky. Timothy lost his sense of direction and was about to ask how much farther they had to go, when Sam stopped suddenly and shone his torch twice. An answering beam shone from the doorway of a building opposite. The boys went towards it.

'Nice work,' said Sam to the look-out. 'Keep your eyes skinned for the cops and drop the bucket down the area steps if you see one of their cars coming. Then scarper. We'll get out the back way.'

Timothy peered up at the soot-grimed walls. In the feeble lamp light he could see that most of the window panes were either broken or missing, and that what had once been an imposing front entrance was now boarded up.

Sam, who knew the geography of the place well, led Timothy down some crumbling stone steps and knocked twice on the basement door. Nobby opened it, flashed his torch and grinned. 'He's come then. Didn't think you'd get this little fly into the spider's parlour.'

'You shut your big mouth, Nobby,' retorted Sam. 'Is everybody here?' Nobby jerked a thumb over his shoulder. 'All set.'

The scene that met Timothy's gaze would have startled even the most stout-hearted. The basement cellar was eerie, the only light coming from candles stuck in bottles. Here and there boys squatted on upturned crates. Others moved restlessly from one spot to another, their pale faces momentarily illumined by the flickering, yellow light.

In the middle, like a set stage piece, two enormous empty casks had been mounted on heavy wooden chests. On the floor below the right-hand cask lay a tattered flock-filled mattress. Suddenly Jake picked up a broad plank and placed it in position between the barrels. Then he took from his pocket a thick, brown scarf.

Timothy eyed it suspiciously. 'What's that for?'

'To blindfold you,' explained Jake, waving a hand towards the raised barrels. 'You're going to walk the plank and jump on to the mattress.' He grinned. 'You know, like the old-time sailors used to do. Everyone here has done it at some time or another. And we'll be

47

on either side to catch you if you wobble and fall. You aren't going to chicken out on us, are you?'

Timothy shook his head. 'No, but it seems a daft sort of idea to me.' With Jake's help he climbed a rickety pair of steps and, once on the plank, allowed himself to be blindfolded. Then very carefully, putting one foot gingerly in front of the other, he began inching his way across. All at once there was a loud clatter down the steps outside. The boys froze, then with a shout of 'Cops' they stampeded towards a back door.

Timothy whipped off the scarf and found himself in complete darkness. Unnerved, he was incapable of moving. Then to his relief a powerful torch pin-pointed him and a moment later a strong, but none too gentle arm jerked him to safety.

'You stupid young idiot,' said the constable. 'Haven't you the sense you were born with?'

Timothy tried to explain that it was just part of a ceremony.

'Ceremony, my foot!' exclaimed the constable flashing his torch to where the mattress should have been. 'If you'd reached the end of the plank and jumped, you'd have landed in a barrel of cold water and probably broken your ankle as well.'

Timothy stared as if he could not believe his eyes.

Then he said: 'The dirty, rotten creeps. They won't catch me out a second time.'

'It's tonight I'm concerned about,' broke in the constable. 'Breaking and entering, that's what the charge should be.' He tapped his teeth with the handle of his torch. 'But as you seem to be more victim than villain, I'm inclined to let you off – on one condition. I want the names of the ringleaders.'

Timothy looked up at the burly policeman. 'I'm sorry, Constable. I'd . . . I'd rather not. If I grass on them, it'll only mean more trouble for me.'

The constable snapped his notebook shut and sighed. 'Grass on them. You've even picked up the lingo. But you could be right. So up the stairs with you and into the police car. I'll have to follow my own hunch. But I hope when I tell my side of the story that your dad whacks a little sense into your backside.'

# 5
# A family for Tiptoes

'You'd think they'd feel sorry for me,' Timothy said, when for the third day running his parents had refused to let him visit his sick pet. 'If I'd broken my ankle as Constable Rogers said I might, they wouldn't have been so mean.' He stepped off the balcony and re-entered the sitting-room.

'But you didn't,' said Betty, following him, 'and you did break into the warehouse. That makes you as bad as Jake and his gang.'

Timothy glowered at her. 'You needn't rub it in. I honestly thought they wanted to be friends. Whose side are you on, anyway?'

'Tiptoes'. That's why I've been to the shop each day to see how he was. Don't you want to know if he's better?'

Timothy could hardly bring himself to say 'yes', because the news for the past two days had been so bad. Tiptoes had neither eaten nor drunk.

'His one-eyed cold has gone at last,' Betty went on,

'and Mr Brent is letting him out for a free flight on Saturday with some of his older pigeons. They'll help bring him back to his new loft. After that his real training will begin.'

Tiptoes' first taste of real freedom lasted an hour. Timothy stood tense with apprehension every time a pigeon returned and only relaxed when at last his pet alighted on the landing platform. All hopes and plans for serious training, however, had to be postponed. Early December brought bitter winds and hard frosts. The water in the drinking trough froze and the pigeons huddled closely together for warmth. In the skyscraper flats the wind howled round the windows and in spite of central heating, Gran spoke longingly of the open coal fires she used to enjoy. Mr Marshall began to dread the early and late night turn on his bus, and Timothy walked to school with numbed fingers and toes.

Worse was to follow, for before long the lift to the sixteenth floor was also put out of action, and every light bulb on every landing was stolen or smashed by vandals.

Groups of them waited in the dark corridors to pounce on the unwary, and Gran, who was one of them, was again forced to do noble battle with her umbrella. She stumbled into the flat with her hat askew and her fists clenched. But although her eyes were still alight with the spark of battle, Timothy noticed that she did not venture out again for a week. The police came and went. Gran enjoyed answering questions, but although her hazy descriptions suggested that the ringleaders might have been Jake and Nobby, there was no real proof.

Timothy wondered how he, himself, had escaped, but his peace was to be shortlived. On the day the lifts were mended and frost gave way to driving snow, he and Betty became targets for a snowball attack as they

left Mr Brent's shop. The first caught Betty on the side of her head and brought tears to her eyes. The second, hard packed as a miniature cannon ball, landed on Timothy's chin and left a scarlet weal. A third momentarily blinded him, and before he could retaliate the gang was upon them.

Jake wasted no time. 'Come on, hand it over,' he said, juggling with a couple of snowballs.

Timothy dashed the snow from his eyes and felt Betty's hand slide into his. 'Hand what over?' he asked.

'The lovely lolly, of course,' said Nobby. 'We all know you do odd jobs for Mr Brent and that Saturday is pay day. And you always share with your friends, you know that, Pigeon-Toes.'

Timothy's heart was racing, but he stood his ground. 'Friends! A fine lot of friends you turned out to be. So push off. You're not getting a penny piece and you can stop calling me Pigeon-Toes.'

'We'll see about that,' said Jake, raising his arm. 'You haven't got your gran lurking in the background this time.'

The next instant the ammunition was knocked from his grasp. 'Lay off,' said Sam. 'Pelting the kids with snow is one thing, but Pigeon-Toes has earned that money, and you're not going to pinch it.' Warding off

Jake and aiming a kick at Nobby's shins, Sam jerked his head in the direction of Peacock Building. 'Beat it, both of you.'

Timothy and Betty could hardly believe their ears, but they needed no second invitation. They ran and did not stop until both were safely in the lift.

Timothy pressed the button to the sixteenth floor. 'Funny!' he said. 'I can't make Sam out. One moment he does the dirty on you, and the next he turns on his own gang.'

In the weeks that followed Timothy forgot the incident. There were brief glimpses of Jake and Sam, but neither spoke nor made any friendly or unfriendly gestures. The snow disappeared and the whipping wind changed to a more southerly direction. In the park where Tiptoes was now taken regularly for trial flights the daffodil blades were two inches above the ground, and almost before Timothy realised it, it was St Valentine's Day. Fortunately it fell on a Saturday and on Mr Marshall's rest day.

'This is Tiptoes' wedding day,' Timothy announced solemnly at breakfast. 'You will come, won't you, Dad? You haven't seen Blue Haze yet.'

'Wouldn't miss it for anything.' His father winked at his wife. 'Like us to bring a bag of confetti?'

'And a wedding cake,' added his mother.

'Come off it,' said Timothy. 'You're kidding.'

'We're not,' put in Gran. 'Time we had something to celebrate. Goodness knows, I've been penned up in this zoo long enough.'

So at six o'clock in the evening after the pet shop was closed, the entire Marshall family arrived at Mr Brent's primrose-painted door. Although he was surprised to see them, his welcome was warm. Mrs Marshall carried the iced cake into the back yard while Timothy filled an earthenware bowl with chips and straw and watched while Mr Brent introduced Tiptoes and Blue Haze to their new nesting compartment. Gran tossed a handful of confetti into the air and, after cutting the cake into five slices, Timothy tossed a few crumbs through the bars of the pigeon loft.

'How long will it take for the babies to hatch?' he asked.

Mr Brent laughed and licked his finger free from icing. 'What a lad! Your name ought to be Mr Impatient. You're counting your chickens even before the eggs have been laid.'

Nevertheless, Timothy could not help being impatient. Day succeeded day and still Blue Haze strutted about the floor of the loft. Then on the eighth day when he and Betty called in on the way home from school, his suspense was ended. Blue Haze, with Tiptoes standing at her side, was no longer strutting and pecking, but sitting sleepy-eyed and contented on her nest.

Timothy turned to Mr Brent. 'Has she really and truly laid an egg?'

Mr Brent nodded. 'And she'll lay another about four o'clock the day after tomorrow.'

Timothy danced about the yard and almost fell headlong into the tub of bathing water. 'Tiptoes is a father! Tiptoes is a father!' he sang out.

'Pipe down, lad,' warned Mr Brent. 'You don't want

to scare her. And remember what I said before. Eggs can become addled, you know.'

No such misfortune befell Blue Haze. The incubation period passed uneventfully. Each parent shared the duty of keeping the eggs warm, and on the eighteenth day the eggs began to chip. When Timothy and Betty next peered through the loft bars, the broken shells lay on the floor and two little balls of grey-blue fluff crouched low in the nest.

'Oh, aren't they lovely,' cried Betty, 'and doesn't Tiptoes look proud.'

Mr Brent went to a box and shook the metal rings inside it. 'Choose your numbers, Tim, and in eight days' time we'll ring them and register your family in the local club secretary's register.'

Timothy's eyes shone, then shutting them tightly he picked up two metal rings. '4K 76845 and 86J 5968. What big numbers for such tiny babies. These really do make me a pigeon fancier, don't they?'

'Aye, lad, they do,' answered Mr Brent kindly, 'but only time will tell whether you've got a champion.'

# 6
## Tiptoes plays truant

More surprises were in store for Timothy for, like all the newly born, Tiptoes' family had to be fed. And since babies could not digest the hard maple peas and tic beans, Tiptoes and Blue Haze took it in turns to grind the food up into pigeon milk and pump it into the ever-open mouths.

Timothy and Betty watched fascinated and were amazed how quickly the babies grew. At fourteen days old they had spiky, undergrown feathers and looked ragged. At this stage they were called 'squeakers' because of the noise they made whenever they were hungry. At twenty days old, although fully feathered, they were still not flying and neither had made any effort to leave the nest.

If anything, Tiptoes seemed the prouder of the two parents and he was for ever hovering nearby, showing his babies how to preen their feathers and how to try and pick up their own food. Blue Haze, on the other hand, seemed restless. 'She wants a race, does that one,' said Mr Brent. 'Pigeons get bored if they're cooped up too long. Tell you what, we'll race them together.' He rang up a friend and, finding that there were two short races billed for the following Saturday, chose the one from Guildford. Mr Brent himself was to be responsible for driving the entrants to the starting place.

Timothy's eyes grew round. 'All the way from Guildford!' he cried. 'Blue Haze might make it. But Tiptoes won't. He's never flown much farther than from the nearest park. He'll get lost. I know he will.'

Timothy's voice sounded more and more distressed and Mr Brent had some difficulty in quietening him. 'The decision's entirely yours, Tim,' he began. 'But if you want Tiptoes to be a real racer, he's got to begin young, and now, or he'll never be ready for his first race from the Channel Islands in April or May.' Giving Timothy a little shake, he went on, 'Don't worry so, lad. Tiptoes is a father, remember. He'll be so anxious to get back to his babies, he'll be jet propelled and so will Blue Haze. We'll release them together.'

Far from happy, Timothy gave his reluctant consent. 'How do I get to Guildford?' he asked, thinking of the fare and his meagre pocket money.

'You'll be a passenger in my collecting van and so

59

will Betty if she likes to come. There aren't many entries, only about thirty baskets.'

Saturday came at last. The weather was fine and the meteorological office promised a slight head wind, high light cloud and no possibility of rain. By nine o'clock Timothy and Betty sat on stools inside the van and watched the baskets being loaded. Each one was slotted and barred at the side to let air in and to enable a small drinking trough to be fitted. Drinking was limited and only a sprinkling of food trickled in through the lids, because, as Mr Brent explained, overfed birds would not fly. He glanced at his watch. 'That's odd,' he remarked. 'Sam's father said he was racing. Not like him to be late. I wonder if he's mistaken the collecting point and taken his pigeons over to Joe. Perhaps I'd better telephone and make sure.'

Mr Brent shut the van door leaving Betty and Timothy surrounded by quietly cooing, fluttering birds. It was an oddly soothing sound and Timothy began to feel happier about the race. After all, Blue Haze would be with Tiptoes, and it was well known that practised racers helped beginners to keep on course.

As he was thinking this, the van door opened and Sam climbed inside carrying his own travelling basket. 'Hello,' he said. 'Very nearly didn't make it.

First, Dad couldn't decide which of his champions to enter, then at the last moment he has to go and rick his ankle. So I'm here instead.'

Timothy and Betty remained silent. Neither was quite sure that the old animosities had gone. Sam was unabashed. 'You two here for the ride?'

'No,' said Timothy. 'I'm racing Tiptoes and Blue Haze.'

Sam laughed. 'What, those little pip-squeaks of birds I've seen you training in the park. You haven't a hope. Especially with Tiptoes. Feed him up a bit and he might just about stagger home from the Guildford run next year. Good job for you this is only a pre-season trial and not recorded.' He patted the lid of his own basket. 'Now take my dad's Mealy. He's a sure fire winner.'

In spite of his annoyance, Timothy began to giggle. 'What a name for a pigeon. Wouldn't give mine a name like that.'

''Tisn't a name, you twit,' Sam replied scornfully. 'It's a breed. A Mealy is a fawnish colour with reddish bars. A beauty. And I'll tell you something else. My dad's Mealy has already won the Champion's race from Nantes four times running. He's entering again this year. Roughly seven hundred and sixty miles. Think of

61

that. Takes all of three days before he gets home. When Tiptoes can match that you can call him a racing pigeon.' He grinned. 'As it is, even on this short run, you should keep him safely in his basket. You don't know anything, and you don't stand a chance.'

'At least keep your big mouth shut,' shouted Timothy.

Betty, who was afraid the argument might end in blows, told Timothy not to get upset. 'He's just a great big show-off.'

'A show-off, am I? Well, today will prove something; not much, I admit. To give your Tiptoes a chance I'll handicap my Mealy. Tiptoes can have a quarter of an hour's start, and if he gets home an hour later than mine, I'll buy him a sack of tic beans. If not, you buy me a sack. How's that for a deal? Willing to take it?'

As he said this the van door opened. Mr Brent looked from one flushed face to the other. He did not look very pleased. 'I understand you're taking your father's place, Sam,' he began, 'but when I say assemble at nine o'clock, I mean nine. Furthermore, as you and Tim don't seem to be enjoying each other's company, I'll have you beside me in front, Sam.'

Sam scowled. 'What, and run the risk of Tim putting

my Mealy out of the race by releasing his own pigeons ten miles this side of the starting point?'

Mr Brent looked really angry this time. 'One more stupid remark from you, my lad, and I'll have you and your dad's pigeons banned from racing for the rest of the season.'

Sam tried to brazen it out with a smile. 'Hey, come off it, Mr Brent. Can't anyone take a joke round here?'

'Not that sort of joke.' Mr Brent settled into the driving seat, and with Sam beside him released the hand brake. The journey to Guildford was quick and smooth. The stopping place was a high spot on the downs overlooking the cathedral. As this was not an official race, the time of release and arrival were only to be recorded by the local club.

The thirty baskets were lined up in a row, and with the latching straps already undone, Mr Brent kept his eye on the minute hand of his watch. At exactly eleven o'clock the lids were lifted and the birds rose in the air in a curving mass of steel grey, blue and whitish-pink feathers. It was impossible to pick out Tiptoes or Blue Haze. They swerved a little to the east, then broke up into little groups of threes and fours until finally all were lost to sight.

Mr Brent poured out hot coffee from a flask and handed round ham rolls. Sam, Betty and Timothy ate hungrily, but at the back of Timothy's mind was the thought that they ought not to be wasting time like this. As if reading his thoughts, Mr Brent smiled and said: 'Don't worry, Tim. However long we kept our foot on the accelerator and broke the speed rules, the birds would be home before us. And there's someone at each home to record the time of arrival.'

'I told him he didn't know anything,' said Sam.

'Neither did you when you started,' Mr Brent reminded him, 'and I'd think more of you if you tried rearing a bird of your own instead of relying on your father's successes. It's easy to crow about someone else's prizes. I'll be the first to applaud when one of your very own pigeons breaks a record.'

The reprimand, although kindly given, had the desired effect. Sam did not say another word throughout the homeward journey, and when at last they tumbled out of the van at Mr Brent's shop, he did not even wait to say goodbye.

Mr Brent, on the other hand, went about unloading the van quietly and methodically. Then finally he led the youngsters into the back yard. A neighbour, who had been keeping watch out of a back window, hesitated and then said: 'All home except two, and very good time they all made.'

Timothy did not need to ask who the missing two were. 'I knew it,' he burst out, 'and I was right. Tiptoes is still too young to go racing. Why, it's all of forty miles from here to Guildford.'

'But Blue Haze is a trained racer,' said Mr Brent behind him. 'Plenty of time yet. We'll give them until sunset.'

Timothy and Betty refused the meal the pigeon fancier offered. Instead they paced the small back yard and stared at the sky until their eyes ached. At last there was nothing left to do but to go home. Timothy slept little that night, and when he did, the shrill ringing of the telephone bell woke him. His voice was drowsy as he answered Mr Brent.

'Come over, Tim,' said the pet shop owner. 'Something to show you.'

Forgetting that he had promised to make his father and mother an early cup of tea, Timothy raced to the shop as fast as his legs would carry him. Once in the yard, Mr Brent nodded towards the sycamore tree growing next door. 'Look up there,' he said. 'Too ashamed to show themselves properly, I reckon.'

Timothy peered up through the fresh spring green

and there, huddled close together, were Tiptoes and
Blue Haze. Mr Brent laughed. 'Do you know what I
think, Tim? I think those two rascals have been having
a bit of a holiday. It's hard work rearing babies, and I
shouldn't have let Blue Haze race with Tiptoes. They
like each other too much.'

'How do we get them down?' asked Timothy,
grinning all over his face.

Mr Brent led the way back into the house. 'Stay
behind the curtains and watch,' he said. 'When the
coast is clear, they'll let themselves in by their own front

door.' A few minutes passed and then it happened exactly as the pet shop owner had said it would.

'Well, Tim, do we scold them and put them on short rations?' he asked with a twinkle in his eye.

'I guess not,' replied Tim. 'I guess they both deserve a day off now and again.'

# 7
## Tiptoes on trial

At twenty-eight days Tiptoes' babies left the nest and began to fend for themselves. Mr Brent removed them to a section of the loft reserved for the very young, and in spite of still being unable to fly, they spent many happy hours flapping from one landing board to another. Then when they were six weeks old the parents' responsibilities were really over. The babies flew free with some of the older birds, and Tiptoes' time was entirely given over to training for his first major race.

'And this time Blue Haze won't be with him,' Mr Brent told Timothy. 'I'm entering him for the Channel Island run, whereas Blue Haze will be on the three to four days race from Bordeaux.'

Timothy whistled in amazement, 'All that way and no one to feed her!'

'Oh, pigeons are quite self reliant. Plenty of seeds and green stuff to eat on the way and plenty of water to quench her thirst. What's more, with the right conditions, I've known pigeons fly fourteen and a half hours non-stop.' Mr Brent's eyes twinkled. 'The only trouble will be if Blue Haze decides she likes France better than she does us.'

Dozens of questions raced through Timothy's mind. Where did the pigeons start from? How were they timed? And so on. Mr Brent explained patiently enough. 'We have collecting points for the big races,' he began, 'then they are driven down in vans to Southampton Docks. There they're fed by the men in charge and given a drink just before all the forms are filled in for the boat people and the Customs Office. After arriving at Cherbourg they have to travel hundreds of miles by road.

'Phew!' exclaimed Timothy. 'Do the same men look after them?'

'Yes, the drivers take it in turn to drive and sleep after every hundred miles.'

Timothy still looked puzzled. 'But how do your officials in London know when the race starts, for timing purposes, I mean?'

'Ah, I wondered when you'd come to that,' said Mr Brent with a smile. 'Sometimes it's difficult to phone England from the Continent, so our people phone through to the French starting place. Weather conditions are given as to winds and likelihood of fog. Then if the conditions hold good, and it's decided to release the birds at six-thirty in the evening, the timing clocks are set. The moment the handle is turned the time is recorded and the race is on. But of course if conditions change, the whole thing is called off or postponed.'

'And each pigeon is checked by its ring number, I suppose,' said Timothy.

'It's a bit more complicated than that,' answered Mr Brent. 'Two check sheets are filled in before departure, giving colour of pigeon, its sex, ring number and race mark. Then the envelope is sealed and handed to the secretary of the federation.'

'I see. That cuts out cheating.' Timothy nodded.

'Another precaution is taken,' broke in Mr Brent, 'one that even the owner doesn't know about. A rubber band bearing a secret number is inserted under the metal ring and recorded by the authorities. This is done well before the point of departure.'

'Will all this apply to Tiptoes?' Timothy sounded a little doubtful.

Mr Brent nodded. 'Now comes a big decision for you. Tiptoes can either cross to Guernsey by boat from Weymouth, or travel by air from London Airport in an aerated cardboard box. I need hardly add that the journey will be much shorter. Also you can travel in my van to London Airport and wave him goodbye.'

'London Airport every time,' said Tim. 'Can Betty come too? I know she tags along rather a lot, but I did sort of promise if there was a chance.'

'Of course,' said Mr Brent. 'I must warn you though. There will be two other passengers. Sam's father is in charge of the long run from Bordeaux, but he's testing six of his younger birds out on the run from Guernsey. He's given one to Sam and one to Jake. Get them interested in pigeon racing and they might be a lot less of a nuisance.'

Timothy could not object. The van belonged to Mr

Brent and he could choose his own passengers. Nevertheless, when the day came he viewed the journey with some apprehension. Jake watched him out of the corner of his eye and so did Sam, and as the birds were ringed with the secret numbers, Timothy had to admit that every one of the six birds they entered looked a prize-winner.

Jake was the first to break the silence. 'You've got quite a good-looker there, Tim, even though Sam seems to think he's a bit undersized. Don't know much about pigeons myself. I'm really coming for the ride and a look at the planes. Gosh! Wouldn't it have been smashing if we could have flown out to Guernsey with them. I bet they'll take ages to get back.'

Mr Brent shook his head. 'No, they won't. They'll be freed an hour after landing in Guernsey and be back at their lofts by six o'clock the same evening.'

Jake grinned. 'I shan't be there to see them arrive. I'm going to watch the jets until I'm turned out.'

'I'd rather you didn't,' said Mr Brent.

Jake laughed. 'Don't worry, Mr Brent. Sam and I have done it before, and we've got enough money to get us home.'

'I'd still prefer you to travel back with us. But I warn you, I intend to be back in time to see Tiptoes pick up his first prize.'

Timothy felt the colour rise in his cheeks. 'Now who's counting chickens?'

'I know, I know, but barring accidents, Tiptoes should be among the first home. He's in fine form; he's trained hard and well.' Mr Brent smoothed the pigeon's feathers, and assuring himself that all was well, he closed the lid of Tiptoes' box.

A few minutes later the van was on its way. Timothy felt uneasy in the company of Jake and Sam. He had not forgotten the attacks in the past. But they seemed friendly enough this morning. Mr Brent, on the other hand, was delighted. Betty was a loyal, good friend, but Timothy, he felt, needed boys of his own age.

Despite the heavy traffic along the motorway, the journey to London Airport was quick. Timothy stood in one of the loading bays and looked skywards. A jet took off with a roar, skimming the rooftops by inches, it seemed. His heart gave a lurch. Soon Tiptoes would be skyborne across the Channel. And when he landed on the other side, there would be no Blue Haze to urge him homewards.

Part of him wanted to call the race off; part of him longed for Tiptoes to do well. As if reading his thoughts, Mr Brent set all of them to help unload the van. He, on the other hand, wandered off to hand in his

papers to the officials, pay the travelling dues and get a
final weather report.

By the time he came back the aerated boxes were
already being loaded aboard a plane. After handing his
clearance papers to the man in charge, he said: 'I envy
you the flight and the race, James. You're going to
have a fast south-west wind. With a three o'clock
release, the birds should all be home by six o'clock.' He
turned to Timothy and Betty. 'By the way, what's
happened to Sam and Jake?'

'Have you forgotten?' said Betty. 'They've gone to

75

watch the jets take off. Jake got impatient and said there was nothing exciting about the loading of pigeons.'

'Well, they won't be allowed nearer than the visitors' point, so we'll give them half an hour, then if they don't turn up, I'll have to accept the fact that they *can* make their own way home.'

Four by four the boxes disappeared aboard the aircraft. The fluttering and the cooing died to a complete silence, as if each bird knew that it must rest before the coming trial of strength.

Timothy looked anxiously up at the sky again where a few pillow-shaped clouds were travelling swiftly across the blue. Mr Brent patted his shoulder. 'They're all going the right way, Tim, so if you start worrying aloud, I'll make you get out and walk home.'

Timothy grinned. Mr Brent made it all sound so easy and straightforward. Of course Tiptoes would be all right, even though he had loitered on the Guildford run. With the final box loaded and the door shut, the three watched the plane taxi along the runway, turn nose into wind, gain speed, then rise like a racing bird itself.

'Goodbye, Tiptoes. Goodbye,' shouted Betty. 'And good luck.' She waved until the plane was no bigger

than a speck. Timothy stood silent. There was something akin to a lump in his throat. He wished now that he had been able to go all the way to Guernsey and bid farewell to his pigeon at the starting point.

He might be puzzled, bewildered or frightened, but whatever his feelings, Tiptoes would be alone with nothing but the sky above and the water below. Timothy knew feelings of this type well. He had them sometimes at the flat and he had them now. In spite of cheerful Mr Brent and chattering Betty, he felt curiously alone.

# 8
## The end of the race

Mr Brent turned away to his now empty van. There was still no sign of Jake or Sam. 'Well, it's their loss,' he remarked. 'I was going to treat them as well as you to a super lunch. After all it isn't every day of the week that we send Guernsey two hundred or so of our best Red Grizzles, Checquers, Mealies, Pieds and Blues. So what shall it be – chicken or. . . .'

'Fish and chips,' said Betty and Timothy together.

'Fish and chips it is then.' Mr Brent guided them through to the cafeteria and at the same time kept a sharp look-out for the missing boys. But soon he was giving full attention to the meal which was crisply cooked and good to taste.

Suddenly Mr Brent grinned. 'No need to gobble, Tim. We shall be home in plenty of time before Tiptoes.' So Timothy slowed down his eating, and capped his meal with an enormous peach sundae and a glass of fizzy lemonade.

Mr Brent grinned again. 'Just as well you aren't flying, my lad, with that lot inside you.'

Betty sucked lemonade through a straw. 'How far will they have got to by now?'

'Almost touching down, I should say.' Mr Brent glanced at his wrist watch. 'Release is at three o'clock. So while I phone through a weather report, you've time to watch a few take-offs and landings. That's if you'd like to. And then we ought to have a last look round for Jake and Sam.'

Timothy sat back with a sigh of satisfaction. 'Just wait until I tell them what they missed. It was a smashing dinner. Thanks a lot, Mr Brent.'

In spite of his anxieties about Tiptoes, Timothy was beginning to enjoy himself. The good food had helped, and so had the bustle and excitement of the place. The sky, too, was a comforting blue.

He and Betty watched the giant planes and put their hands over their ears to shut out some of the noise. They were almost disappointed when Mr Brent returned after a final fruitless search for Jake and Sam to say that they must go.

'Can't we stay just ten minutes more?' pleaded Betty. 'Look at all those bouquets being handed into that plane. Somebody terribly important must be about to take off.'

'Somebody very important has already taken off,'

79

broke in Mr Brent. 'Do you realise that Tiptoes is already flying over the sea and making for home?'

Timothy needed no further persuasion, but when all three were seated in the van, they were dismayed to find that it would not start.

'Odd.' Mr Brent tried again. His van had recently been serviced and it was a trustworthy vehicle. There was no doubt about it, however, the engine was completely dead. Getting out of the van, he lifted the bonnet and peered inside. When he re-appeared the children were quick to sense Mr Brent's anxiety. 'I simply can't understand it,' he said. 'Everything seems to be in good order.' He tried starting the van a third time and at length gave up with a gesture of despair. All at once a mechanic, wiping his hand on an oil cloth, strolled over. 'Having trouble, mate?'

Mr Brent nodded, and surrendered the engine to the man's more experienced eyes and hands. Within two minutes he had located the trouble. 'Someone's pulled a fast one on you, mate, and removed the rotor arm,' he said. 'And whoever it was was clever enough to replace the distributor cover so you wouldn't find out too easily.'

'Removed the rotor arm!' exclaimed Mr Brent. 'Good gracious! Do you get many pretty thefts like this around here?'

'Hundreds,' replied the mechanic. 'You'd be surprised what some people will pinch.'

Mr Brent looked suddenly anxious. 'How long will the repair take?'

'Depends. You'll have to track down a spare, first,' replied the mechanic. 'You'll need to ring the nearby garages and see who's got one. There's a telephone over there.'

Telling the children not to leave the van, Mr Brent went off with the mechanic. Timothy sat silent and his face was unusually pale. Betty tucked her hand into one of his. 'I'm sorry, Tim. I know what you're thinking. But it will be all right, you'll see. Mr Brent will phone the shop, and the man who's helping out will clock our birds in.'

Timothy snatched his hand away. 'There isn't any helper. Mr Brent closed the shop for the day. So unless we get back before the pigeons do, our part of the race is a washout.'

It was two hours before the van was repaired and ready to start, and one glance at Mr Brent's wrist watch was enough to dash all their hopes. With the traffic increasing on the inward run to town, thirty miles an hour was the most he could achieve. More often than not their speed dropped to twenty and there were hold-ups every ten minutes or so.

Timothy sat hunched in a corner of the van, and in spite of all Mr Brent's and Betty's reminders that there were plenty of races still to come before the season ended, he would not be comforted.

At last the van drew up outside the primrose-painted door. Stiffly, Timothy dragged himself to his feet and followed the others through to the yard. As he did so the Town Hall clock struck seven.

Mr Brent went from one youngsters' loft to another,

and silently counted up his racing entries lined up on the landing platforms. Their throbbing, cooing notes voiced a welcome. Betty counted too, and so did Timothy. Then they looked at each other. All had returned safely from the Channel Island race except one. Tiptoes was missing. Unable to find words Betty stared miserably at Timothy. Timothy stared back, then suddenly he burst out. 'I knew he shouldn't have gone on the race. He was too young. And he didn't have Blue Haze to help him. Now he's probably drowned in the sea and I'll never see him again.'

'Have you forgotten all I've told you?' said Mr Brent gently. 'Being overdue for an hour or so in a first race is nothing. Last year two of my beginners took two days to get back from Guernsey. And remember. He's had fine weather all the way.'

'Well, he hasn't now,' said Timothy, lifting his face to a thin drizzle, and feeling the first chill of the wind blowing through his jacket. A sob almost broke through into his voice. 'I should never have listened to you. If . . . if he doesn't get back, I'll . . . I'll never forgive you.' So saying he turned on his heels and fled from the yard.

Close to tears herself, Betty looked up at Mr Brent. 'I'm sorry. I'm sure he doesn't mean it. It's because he's upset.'

'I know. No, I shouldn't go after him if I were you, Betty. Best leave him alone for a bit.'

Betty, however, was deaf to this advice. If Tim was in trouble and upset her place, she felt, was at his side. Outside the shop she looked first to the right and then to the left. Under the pall of heavy black clouds twilight seemed to have come especially early. Of one thing she was certain. In his present state of mind, Timothy would not go home.

She thought of all his familiar haunts – the park – the hut on the allotment and searched each in turn. Finally she turned into the road where Timothy used to live. Not a house was standing, but here and there in the back yard a tool shed or a coal shed still stood intact.

Suddenly illumined in a pool of light from one of the street lamps she saw Timothy. He was slumped against the post as if he needed its support to keep him upright. Betty hurried to his side. 'Oh, Tim, I've been searching everywhere for you.' She peered a little closer. 'You aren't sick, are you?'

He nodded. 'I expect it was the chips and the ice cream and the van ride and everything.'

Betty thought quickly and remembered that in Tim's old yard there was an outside water tap. She wondered if it still worked. Tugging Timothy by the arm she steered him through the crazily hanging back door. Stepping gingerly over the piles of fallen rubble, they reached the tap and turned it on. A trickle of water rewarded them, but it was enough to revive Timothy. All at once as he drank from cupped hands there was the sound of low, contented cooing.

Betty and Tim turned sharply and looked towards the old pigeon loft that Timothy's father had built. Part of the landing stage was broken, but the little flap door still swung on its hinges. Inside, something grey and soft, with grey-blue wing feathers moved from side to side.

Timothy gave a loud cry, and a moment or two later Tiptoes was cradled lovingly between his two hands and nuzzling at his cheek.

'You made it. You made it!' Timothy cried, 'even if you did forget which is your real home now.'

'Oh, Tim!' Betty was half crying, half laughing. 'I knew clever old Tiptoes would get home. Come on. Let's go and tell Mr Brent.'

The two children hurriedly retraced their steps, but when Mr Brent opened the primrose-painted door, he was not alone. Sam stood beside him. Timothy ignored him. 'I've found him! I've found him!' he shouted. 'The old silly flew back to his old home.'

Sam's face momentarily brightened. 'Tim, I am glad. It makes me feel sort of better.'

Timothy looked puzzled. 'What's it got to do with you? I know he lost the race but . . .'

'Go on, Sam, tell him,' broke in Mr Brent. 'Tell him just as you told me.'

Sam hung his head, then suddenly looked Timothy straight in the eye. 'It was Jake's idea, not mine, honest it wasn't. He stole the rotor arm.'

'Jake did that! Whatever for?' asked Timothy.

'To delay you, so that neither you nor Mr Brent would be able to tell what time Tiptoes and the others finished the race.'

'And you let him do it.' Tim's voice was scornful. 'You rotten twister.'

Sam nodded. 'But I came to own up and say I'm sorry. I'll never do anything like that again.'

'And I suppose it was Jake who hid Tiptoes in his old loft where he could have starved to death.'

'Oh, no, Tim.' Sam's voice was horrified. 'Jake wanted you to lose the race, but the rest was Tiptoes' idea.'

'I don't believe you.'

'I didn't expect you would,' said Sam. 'But young birds do sometimes get confused and it isn't all that long since you moved into the flat. Isn't that right, Mr Brent?'

Mr Brent nodded. 'I think you must give Jake the benefit of the doubt. Sam's quite right. Such things do happen, though no one can exactly say why.' He turned to Sam. 'All the same that doesn't let you and Jake off the hook. You robbed me and possibly Tim of the chance of winning a silver cup, and I shall have to report the matter to the club officials. The race will undoubtedly be disqualified, but whether they take the matter further is their concern. I've a mind to get them to overlook your part in the plot because you owned up. What do you say, Tim?'

Timothy looked at Sam and then at Tiptoes. 'Yes, I think we'll let them both off – Sam for getting hooked up with a twister like Jake, and Tiptoes for not remembering his real home address.'

'I don't think Tiptoes deserves a word of blame,' declared Betty. Her eyes were shining. 'He might not have won the cup this time, but he's proved one thing.'

'You're right, Betty, he has,' Timothy said proudly. 'He was put on trial and he won through. He's a racer all right.'